FROM DISNEY'S
THE HUNCHBACK
OF NOTRE DAME

OUT
THERE

MUSIC BY ALAN MENKEN
LYRICS BY STEPHEN SCHWARTZ

NEW YORK

Safe behind these windows and these parapets of stone

Gazing at the people down below me

All my life, I watch them as I hide up here alone

Hungry for the histories they show me

All my life,
I memorize their faces

Knowing them as they
will never know me

All my life, I wonder
how it feels to pass a day

Not above them

But part of them . . .

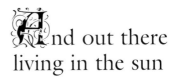nd out there
living in the sun

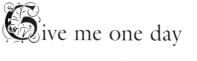

Give me one day
Out there

All I ask is one
to hold forever

Out there

Where they all live
unaware

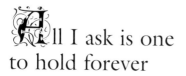

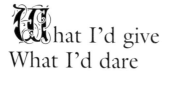hat I'd give
What I'd dare

Just to live one day
out there . . .

ut there among the millers and the weavers and their wives

    Through the roofs and gables

  I can see them

Ev'ry day they shout and scold and go about their lives

Heedless of the gift it is to be them

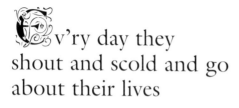

If I was in
their skin

I'd treasure
ev'ry instant

ut there

Strolling by
the Seine

Taste a morning

ut there

Like ordinary men

Who freely walk about there

21-70
71

*J*ust one day and
then I swear

I'll be content

With my share

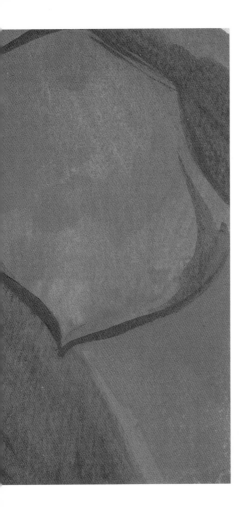

Won't resent
Won't despair

Old and bent
I won't care

I'll have spent
One day

Out there

For information address Hyperion,
114 Fifth Ave., New York, NY 10011

Produced by:
·Welcome Enterprises, Inc., 575 Broadway,
New York, NY 10012

Design by Jon Glick

ISBN 0-7868-6224-6

10 9 8 7 6 5 4 3 2 1

Printed in Singapore by Tien Wah Press